KAY THOMPSON'S *ELOISE*

Eloise Breaks Some Eggs

STORY BY **Margaret McNamara**

ILLUSTRATED BY **Tammie Lyon**

Aladdin Paperbacks

NEW YORK · LONDON · TORONTO · SYDNEY

ALADDIN PAPERBACKS
An imprint of Simon & Schuster Children's Publishing Division
1230 Avenue of the Americas
New York, NY 10020
Art direction and design by Cheshire Studio
The text of this book was set in Century Old Style.
Manufactured in the United States of America
First Aladdin Paperbacks edition January 2005
6 8 10 9 7
Library of Congress Cataloging-in-Publication Data
McNamara, Margaret.
Eloise breaks some eggs / written by Margaret McNamara ;
illustrated by Tammie Speer-Lyon.—1st ed.
p. cm. — (Kay Thompson's Eloise) (Ready-to-read)
Summary: Eloise's cooking lesson with Nanny and Cook is
disastrous—or would be, if Eloise could not order room service.
ISBN 0-689-87368-9 (pbk.)
[1. Cookery—Fiction.]
I. Lyon, Tammie, ill. II. Title. III. Series. IV. Series: Ready-to-read.
PZ7.M47879343El 2005
[E]—dc22
2004008891

I am Eloise.
I am six.

I am a city child.
I live in a hotel
on the tippy-top floor.

This is Nanny.

She is my nanny.
My mother is mostly away.

"Eloise," says Nanny.
"It is time for your lesson."

I ask, "Piano?"
Nanny says, "No."

I ask, "French?"
Nanny says, "No."

I ask, "Poker?"
Nanny says, "No, no, no."

"It is time for
your cooking lesson.

"Today you will cook eggs."

"I do not like to cook,"
I say.

"You like to break things,"
Nanny says.

"You break eggs
to cook them."

I say, "Let's go, go, go."

We take the elevator to the kitchen.

I press every button.

"Today we will cook eggs,"
says the cook.

A bowl can make
a very good hat.
"No, no, no," says Nanny.

"Watch me," says the cook.
The cook is good.

"Now you try," he says.

I am very good.

"NO! NO! NO!" says Nanny.

"You broke the bowl!
You broke the plate!"
says the cook.

I say,
"I broke the eggs, too."

Nanny and
I take the elevator
to the tippy-top floor.
I press every button.

"You will never be a cook,"
says Nanny.
"How will you eat?"

I say, "Room service."
I pick up the phone.
I say, "It's me, Eloise.

"Two eggs,
   and charge it, please.
Thank you very much."